Kisses on The Wind

A Note from the Author:

At some time, most people will find themselves missing
someone they love. It may be someone you don't see as
often as you'd like because they are far away –
such as a dear relative, grandparent or friend. Some miss
those living in a foreign country or serving in the military.
Others miss people they loved years ago but lost touch over the years.
And many mourn the loss of a beloved pet or deceased loved one.
There *IS* a way to reach out to them.
You can send your love to them with your kisses on the wind.

Hide and Seek

Can you find the Little People hiding within these pages?
Native American lore tells of the elusive Little People,
playful spirits who live in nature. They often help
people who are lost or sad.
Folks say that if you think that you see something but when
you look again... there is nothing there!
Or when you are fishing and something tugs on your line,
but when you pull it in you find nothing or a just a stick?
That is the Little People playing tricks on you!
Also, hidden inside these paintings are insects and animals.
Seek and see if you can find the creatures listed at the bottom of the page.
Happy hunting!

Kisses on The Wind

(For those who believe)

Written by Meg Kappel
Illustrated by Samantha Silvas

It is said that many years ago in a Native American village near here there lived two families who were the best of friends. One couple had a baby girl named Sequoia, after the majestic redwood trees of the West. The other couple named their baby boy Mohe, after the swift and strong Elk that roamed the plains.

         ** Two monarch butterflies, gray squirrel, birds flying, and two dogs.

The two families spent many happy years together and Sequoia and Mohe were great friends and often played together in their village. Their proud parents would watch them playing, smile and said "Perhaps one day they will be husband and wife."

**Male and female wild turkeys, a black crow, and birds flying in the distance

Sequoia and Mohe loved nature and felt as one with it: feeling the warmth of the sun on their faces, hearing the wind in the trees, running through the wild fields, and fishing and swimming in the river. They made up a game called "Free the Seeds" and planted the seeds from their food and flowers so they might grow into beautiful plants.

** A gray fox and a bird flying in the distance

    They took care to honor the animals and creatures that lived there. One of their favorite pastimes were nature adventures – taking long walks into nature where they would be as quiet as mice; barely speaking (and whispering when they did), carefully tip-toeing to quietly sneak up on wildlife to watch the animals without frightening them.

                 ** Three blue eastern tail butterflies, mother goose and goslings and flies

As teenagers, Sequoia and Mohe often went on nighttime nature adventures. They would spend hours laughing at each other's funny stories or just gazing with wonder at the beauty of the starlit sky.

** A pair of male and female mallard ducks, and lightning bugs

They spoke of their ancestors who had died but now lived amongst the stars in The Land of Ancestors. Their love for each other grew even more, day by day.

** A turtle, a fish, lightning bugs, and a male deer

As is the custom, when Mohe became a man, he built his own home, one that he and his wife would share once they were married. While the Medicine Woman looked on, he carefully built the home so that it would give them good shelter and keep them warm in the winter. When his home was finished, he was ready to marry.

** An owl, a crow, a mouse, and birds flying

Mohe knew which maiden he wanted to be his wife. Sequoia had always been his best friend. So, with the approval of their parents and the tribal chief, Mohe asked Sequoia to be his wife. Sequoia did not hesitate for a moment: she said yes!

** A spider web and spider, a bird flying in the distance

The evening of their wedding was the greatest celebration. The entire village rejoiced in this marriage of life-long best friends. There was a grand feast with music, singing and dancing. All thanked the Great Spirit for this most wonderful marriage.

** Lightning bugs and a dog

On their wedding night, Mohe and Sequoia moved into the home that Mohe had built. For years they lived there happily as husband and wife. Their life together was full of love and happiness. They appreciated all the wonders of nature that surrounded them. When they ate it was their custom to thank the Great Spirit for the food and then they also thanked each item that they ate. They'd say things like "Thank you, fish, for giving us nourishment. Thank you corn, for giving us your strength. Thank you bread for giving us health."   ** Owl and three fish

They still played "Save the Seeds" - saving and planting their seeds and saw that many of the seeds that they had planted as children were growing all around them. At night, as darkness fell, they would sit by their fire and watch the fireflies dance. In the darkness the black sky filled with stars. The wind whispered its secrets to the trees. They appreciated the beauty of nature and gave thanks for it all.

**Three fish, a walkingstick, lightning bugs and a dog

But there was trouble in the nation. It was a time of fierce battles and the men from the village were going off to fight. The village elders told young Mohe that he was strong and that in the spring he must go with them to fight in the war. Mohe would have to leave his wife safely behind in their village home.

** Three horses

The young couple's love was great, greater than many. On the day before Mohe had to leave they went on a picnic. The strong brave picked white clover flowers and wove them into a chain. He made a clover necklace for his beloved Sequoia to wear as a reminder of their love until he returned.

** A snail and a beaver

Mohe left to fight in the war. Sequoia stayed behind and wore the clover necklace every day because it made her feel close to Mohe. But her beloved husband would never return.

** Birds flying in the distance

The war was won, but Mohe was lost. Mohe had fought bravely, but he died in battle. Sequoia was heartbroken and although it seemed like she would cry forever, Sequoia knew that a thousand tears would not bring Mohe back to her, for he had crossed over into The Land of Ancestors in the faraway stars.

** A flying bald eagle and a horse

Many moons passed, yet still Sequoia's heart was heavy, and she wore the clover chain of their love. It seemed that her sadness would never go away. She still longed for her life-long friend and husband.

**Nine lightning bugs

The Medicine Woman was wise. She saw Sequoia crying and said to her "Sequoia, as long as you keep mourning for Mohe, he will never be free to join our ancestors in the sky. Our loved ones live on, but they wait for the time when we can let them go. When you think of your beloved, don't ask him to stay behind. Instead, it is better to send your love to him with your kisses on the wind." Sequoia knew that the wise woman was right. It was time to let her sorrow go, to free her beloved. For you see, her sadness and the dried clover necklace kept him chained to her. ** Two ladybugs, a rabbit, a crow, and a skunk

   That night Sequoia had a special dream. In her dream she visited The Land of Ancestors. Mohe was there and they were so happy to be together again. The love between them had never died. At first, they used words to talk to each other but soon words drifted away, and they spoke in thoughts. Without saying a word Sequoia and Mohe understood each other perfectly. They hugged and laughed and "talked" for what seemed like hours and hours. As her dream ended, they hugged good-bye and Sequoia knew that Mohe's love would always be with her.

** A turtle, a fish, lightning bugs, and a male deer

W hen she awakened at dawn, she remembered her special dream. Sequoia took her necklace and one by one, carefully planted the flowers in Mother Earth. As she covered them with the soil, she cried and her tears watered each one. She genuinely loved and missed him. She said, "My beloved husband, I will always remember you, but my love for you is greater than my pain and so I am sending my love to you, with my kisses on the wind."

** Birds flying in the distance

    Something magical began to happen! The dried flowers had seeds in them (as all flowers do). Her tears fell and watered the seeds. The clover seeds quickly sprouted and began to grow beneath the earth. The new sprouts pushed their way up through the soil and tiny green leaves grew. As the clover grew taller, tiny buds formed and then white flowers bloomed. While she watched in amazement, the white flowers changed from white to pink to show that Sequoia's love had freed her beloved Mohe at last.

** A yellow swallowtail butterfly, a caterpillar, two walkingsticks, a ladybug, two snails, two earthworms and birds

Mohe was watching from The Land of Ancestors.

He received Sequoia's loving kisses on the wind and their love was complete.

** Four dragonflies and birds flying

Over the years, those pink clovers had seeds and then those flowers made even more seeds and flowers. As Brother Wind blew the seeds across the plains, they grew into great fields filled with those delicate pink flowers.

**A female deer and birds flying

Today, these beautiful pink and green fields are a joy to behold, their light fragrance floats on the breeze and gentle animals delight in eating this crunchy, sweet, and nutritious treat.

** Two monarch butterflies, a female deer, a rabbit, a bumblebee, and a mouse

    Look carefully for this special pink clover and when you see it, remember how Sequoia's love set them free to grow and bloom forever. You, too, can play "Free the Seeds". And when you think of your loved ones who may seem so far away, remember that you can always send your love to them, wherever they may be … with *your* kisses on the wind.

    ** Two horses, a rabbit, two yellow swallowtail butterflies, a monarch butterfly, two dogs, and a cat

Kisses on *The Wind*

Would you like to send your love to someone with your kisses on the wind?

List them below:

Members of My Family

_____

_____

_____

Friends, Neighbors, Teachers, Loved Ones and More

_____

_____

_____

Pets and Other Creatures

_____

_____

_____

About the Author

Meg Kappel penned two additional children's stories *Light Angels* and *Dream Fliers*, and three screenplays *Companion*, an extra-terrestrial horror film, *Salisbury Resort*, a rock and roll musical and *Unemployed: It Could Be You*, a television series. Meg grew up in the small community of Linstead on the Severn in Maryland. As a child she had an innate affinity with the outdoors and especially with the Severn River. During the summer she spent all day in or on the river - wading, catching crabs, diving, swimming, and boating with friends.

Meg lives near the Atlantic Coast outside of Rehoboth Beach, Delaware. She has three grown children and gleefully plays with five of her grandchildren who live nearby. Her interests include boating, clamming, reef scuba diving and tending to her extensive gardens. She is a graduate of The University of Maryland with a B.A. in Radio, Television, Video and Film.

Dedication

This book is dedicated to my loved ones - you are truly the wind beneath my wings: Sherry, James, Thomas, Jayme, David, Catalina, Nicholas, Evelyn, Theodore, Ethan, Bert, Beth, Kate, Priscilla, Liz, and Susan. I send my kisses on the wind to you... *forever.*

With gratitude to Eric Wright: the gentleman who makes my dreams come true; without your steadfast assistance this book would never have been published.

Illustrator Samantha Silvas is an artist based out of Coeur d'Alene, Idaho.

www.ingramcontent.com/pod-product-compliance
Lightning Source LLC
Chambersburg PA
CBHW041608120626
46551CB00002B/353